CHRISTMAS in
New York City 2024 - 2025

A Complete Travel Guide to Holiday Attractions, Markets, Events, Maps all Year Seasonal Experiences

by
Allen J. Mack

Disclaimer

Table of Contents

Introduction to Christmas in New York City

Christmas in New York City is truly magical. Every year, millions of visitors flock to the Big Apple to experience its one-of-a-kind blend of holiday traditions, world-famous sights, and larger-than-life decorations that appear to bring the city to life in a way that no other season can. New York transforms into a timeless and modern winter wonderland, with the towering Christmas tree at Rockefeller Center, bustling holiday markets, and twinkling light displays.

Walking through the city streets in December, you'll notice the undeniable energy of the season. Storefronts are decked out in intricate displays, each vying for the title of most impressive holiday windows, while public squares and parks are decorated with festive lights, ice skating rinks, and Christmas trees. There's a buzz in the air as people shop for gifts, attend holiday shows, and simply enjoy the festive atmosphere that extends from uptown to downtown.

The holiday season in New York is truly inclusive. Events such as the Radio City Christmas Spectacular and the enchanting displays at Macy's Santaland attract families looking to experience the magic of the season. Couples can enjoy a more intimate holiday escape, such as ice skating under the stars or snuggling up in a corner café with a cup of hot chocolate. There are plenty of activities for solo travellers and groups of friends, ranging from Christmas markets full of unique gifts to festive concerts and world-class dining.

No matter where you're from or what your holiday traditions are, New York City provides an opportunity to celebrate Christmas in grand style, combining its diverse culture with a festive spirit that brings people from all walks of life together. Whether you come for the iconic sights, the winter festivities, or simply to experience the magic of the city lit up in holiday lights, Christmas in New York is an unforgettable experience that will stay with you long after the season is over.

Now that we've laid the groundwork for what to expect during the holidays in the city, let's look at the individual experiences and must-see sights that make New York City one of the most iconic places to celebrate Christmas.

Iconic Christmas Experiences in NYC

New York City is known for its extravagant Christmas celebrations, which include some of the most iconic holiday sights in the world. The city's streets and landmarks are transformed into a festive playground, providing memories that will last a lifetime. In this chapter, we'll look at the must-see attractions associated with Christmas in New York, each with its unique charm.

The Rockefeller Center's Christmas Tree and Ice Skating

The Rockefeller Center Christmas Tree, located at 45 Rockefeller Plaza, New York, NY 10111, is perhaps New York's most well-known Christmas symbol. Every year, this towering evergreen becomes the focal point of holiday festivities, with its dazzling lights and decorations providing a backdrop for thousands of photographs. The tree lighting ceremony, which is typically held in late November or early December, is a major event that draws people from all over the world and is broadcast live to millions. It officially kicks off the Christmas season in New York and is a must-see if you're in town at the time.

Another must-do New York experience is ice skating at the Rockefeller Center rink, which is right beneath the tree. Skating here, with the towering tree above and the majestic skyscrapers all around you, is a truly magical experience. Whether you're a seasoned skater or a beginner, gliding across the ice at one of the world's most famous rinks is an unforgettable experience. Try to reserve your skate time in advance, as this attraction is extremely popular during the holidays.

Dyker Heights Christmas Lights

Dyker Heights in Brooklyn offers a truly one-of-a-kind and extravagant Christmas light display. This neighbourhood, located between 11th and 13th Avenues and 83rd to 86th Streets, is well-known for its extravagant holiday decorations, which transform entire blocks into dazzling displays of lights, inflatable Santas, reindeer, and other Christmas cheer. The residents here take holiday decorating very seriously, spending thousands of dollars to create a spectacle that draws visitors from all over the world.

The best time to visit Dyker Heights is in the evening, between mid-December and New Year's Eve, when the lights are fully illuminated. Walking through this neighbourhood feels like entering a holiday movie set, with each house attempting to outdo the next. It's an excellent way to enjoy the warmth of a New York Christmas in a more intimate, neighbourhood setting. For those who prefer a guided experience, there are bus tours that take visitors through the most beautifully decorated streets.

Saks Fifth Avenue's Light Show and Holiday Window Displays

Another popular New York Christmas tradition is the Saks Fifth Avenue light show and holiday window displays. This luxury department store, located at 611 5th Ave, New York, NY 10022, goes above and beyond every year, transforming its façade into a dazzling light show synchronized to festive music. The show takes place in the evenings, attracting large crowds who gather in front of the building to watch.

In addition to the light show, Saks Fifth Avenue is well-known for its intricate holiday window displays. Every year, the windows are decorated with a different theme, which usually includes animated figures, sparkling lights, and lavish scenes that tell a festive story. These window displays not only showcase New York's creativity but also serve as a reminder of the city's strong connection to Christmas traditions. Other nearby department stores, such as Bergdorf Goodman and Macy's Herald Square, have stunning windows that are worth seeing as you stroll through the city.

Holiday Lights in New York.

While Rockefeller Center and Saks Fifth Avenue are must-see destinations, there are numerous other places to admire Christmas lights throughout the city. Central Park provides a more natural display, particularly around the Wollman Rink, where the lights reflect off the ice and snow. Fifth Avenue is lined with illuminated trees, holiday decorations, and beautifully decorated storefronts, creating a magical atmosphere ideal for an evening stroll.

The Brookfield Place Winter Garden's Luminaries, located at 230 Vesey St, New York, NY 10281, is one of the newer and quickly becoming popular displays. This indoor light installation features glowing lanterns suspended from the ceiling that change colours in a stunning display, creating a serene and enchanting atmosphere.

Another must-see is Hudson Yards' "Shine Bright" light installation, which is located at 20 Hudson Yards, New York, NY 10001. This newer attraction has over two million lights covering the towering structures of this modern development, with numerous photo opportunities throughout the area. It's an excellent place to get a taste of New York's cutting-edge architecture and holiday spirit.

Conclusion: Embracing the Christmas Spirit in NYC.

From the towering Rockefeller tree to the vibrant neighbourhoods of Dyker Heights, New York City's Christmas experiences are unparalleled. Each iconic sight exemplifies the city's ability to celebrate the holiday spirit on a grand scale while also providing moments of warmth and tradition. Whether you're skating beneath the world's most famous Christmas tree or admiring intricate light displays, these experiences encapsulate what makes New York City one of the best places in the world to celebrate Christmas.

Touring New York's Famous Christmas Markets

New York City's Christmas markets are a beloved tradition, bringing together artisans, food vendors, and holiday enthusiasts in a lively celebration of the season. These markets are more than just a shopping destination; they're places to enjoy the festive atmosphere, try seasonal treats, and find one-of-a-kind, handcrafted gifts. In this chapter, we'll visit the city's most popular Christmas markets, each with its unique blend of charm and holiday cheer.

Union Square Holiday Market is a shoppers' paradise.

The Union Square Holiday Market, located in the heart of downtown Manhattan at Union Square Park (14th Street and Broadway, New York, NY 10003), is one of the city's most popular and established Christmas markets. The market, known for its European-style layout and eclectic mix of vendors, is a shoppers' dream for one-of-a-kind gifts and handmade crafts.

The market typically opens in mid-November and runs until Christmas Eve, giving both locals and tourists plenty of time to explore its offerings. Over 150 vendors offer everything from hand-knitted scarves and artisanal jewellery to intricate ornaments and custom art pieces. The market exudes a festive atmosphere, with warm lighting, decorated stalls, and the sounds of Christmas music filling the air.

One of the market's highlights is the variety of food vendors. You can warm up with a cup of hot cider or eat delicious holiday snacks like German bratwurst, Belgian waffles, and artisanal chocolate. The market's diverse range of vendors ensures that you can sample flavours from all over the world, making it both a culinary journey and a shopping experience.

While Union Square can get crowded, especially on weekends, the market's expansive layout and convenient location make it a must-see for anyone looking to soak up the festive atmosphere of New York's holiday season.

Columbus Circle Holiday Market: *Unique Gifts and Local Crafts.*

The Columbus Circle Holiday Market, located at the entrance to Central Park, just off 59th Street and Central Park West, is another popular destination for both locals and tourists. This market is slightly smaller and more intimate than Union Square, but the quality and atmosphere are equally impressive.

The Columbus Circle market, which opened in early December, is a popular holiday shopping destination for those looking for unique, handmade gifts. It showcases a diverse range of artisans selling everything from fine leather goods and jewellery to home décor and children's products. Many of the vendors are local New Yorkers, allowing you to support small businesses while finding truly unique gifts.

This market, located at the gateway to Central Park, provides a serene backdrop for your holiday shopping. After browsing the stalls, take a stroll through the park's snow-covered pathways, perhaps heading to Wollman Rink for a skate or admiring the views from Bow Bridge. Columbus Circle is an ideal destination for those looking to combine city life with a touch of natural beauty during the holidays, thanks to its shopping options and proximity to the park.

The market also has a variety of gourmet food stalls that serve everything from freshly baked pastries to international street foods, allowing you to grab a snack or a warm drink while shopping. Columbus Circle Holiday Market, with its picturesque setting and high-quality vendors, is the perfect place to find thoughtful gifts and spend a festive day.

Bryant Park Winter Village

Bryant Park's Winter Village, located at 6th Avenue and 42nd Street in New York, NY 10018, is a popular holiday destination. This market is more than just a shopping destination; it's a complete winter wonderland. The Winter Village has over 170 kiosks selling holiday goods and a free ice skating rink, making it a popular destination for families and groups of friends.

The Winter Village opens in late October, giving visitors a head start on their Christmas shopping, and remains open until early January, making it one of the city's longest-running holiday markets. The market is housed in custom-designed kiosks that sell a variety of products such as jewellery, decorative home goods, artisanal foods, and warm winter accessories. Many of the vendors at Bryant Park are small businesses from across the United States, allowing customers to find one-of-a-kind gifts that are difficult to find in traditional stores.

The Bank of America Winter Village Rink, the Winter Village's iconic ice skating rink, serves as the centrepiece. Unlike other rinks in the city, skating here is free (though skate rentals are available for a fee), making it an excellent choice for those looking to enjoy a traditional New York holiday activity without breaking the bank. Skating in the heart of midtown, surrounded by festive market stalls and the towering cityscape, is an experience unlike any other.

Aside from shopping and skating, Bryant Park also has food and drink options to satisfy any craving. Warm up with hot chocolate or mulled wine, or grab a bite to eat at one of the many food kiosks that serve international and seasonal specialities. After a day of skating and shopping, you can unwind by the outdoor fire pits or sit by the park's festively decorated tree.

Grand Central Holiday Fair: *Indoor Festivities*

The Grand Central Holiday Fair is an excellent choice for those looking to escape the winter chill while also enjoying a festive shopping experience. Located inside the historic Grand Central Terminal at 42nd Street and Park Avenue, this market provides a cosy indoor alternative to the city's outdoor markets.

The Grand Central Holiday Fair is typically open from mid-November to Christmas Eve and is one of New York City's few fully indoor holiday markets. Shopping here feels elegant and refined while also being festive, thanks to the grand architecture and beautifully decorated halls. Over 40 vendors sell a carefully curated selection of handmade gifts, ranging from fine jewellery and clothing to art, toys, and holiday decorations.

The Holiday Fair is ideal for visitors who prefer to shop in a warmer, more controlled environment while maintaining the charm and quality of a Christmas market. After shopping, you can admire Grand Central's stunning architecture or eat at one of the Terminal's many restaurants, which range from casual to upscale.

A Shopper's Christmas Wonderland.

New York City's Christmas markets are an important part of the holiday season, providing much more than just a shopping experience. Whether you're looking for unique gifts at Union Square, admiring the peaceful surroundings of Columbus Circle, going for a festive skate at Bryant Park, or escaping the cold inside Grand Central Terminal, each market has its flavour of holiday magic.

Holiday Events and Entertainment

New York City is well-known for its vibrant Christmas season, and the festive events and performances in 2024 look to be nothing short of spectacular. Whether you prefer glitzy theatre productions, magical light displays, or grand parades, the city has a plethora of holiday entertainment options that capture the spirit of the season. In this chapter, we'll walk you through the most iconic events, including practical advice on tickets, access, and booking.

The Radio City Christmas Spectacular features the Rockettes and holiday cheer.

A trip to New York during the holidays is incomplete without seeing the Radio City Christmas Spectacular. This show, held at the historic Radio City Music Hall at 1260 6th Ave, has been a beloved Christmas tradition in the city since 1933. From November 15, 2024, to January 5, 2025, the Rockettes will dazzle audiences with perfectly synchronized high kicks, colourful costumes, and larger-than-life production numbers. The 90-minute show is a visual feast, with standout routines including the "Parade of the Wooden Soldiers" and the heartwarming "Living Nativity." With updated visual effects and cutting-edge production, the show has maintained its timeless appeal while continuing to captivate new generations of audiences.

Ticket prices for the 2024-2025 season range between $49 and $275, depending on the date and seat location. Premium dates near Christmas tend to sell out quickly, so book early through the official Radio City Music Hall website or Ticketmaster. If you're travelling with family, look for special family packs and discounts, particularly for November performances. Weekday shows are generally more available and slightly less expensive for those looking for a quieter experience.

Broadway Holiday Shows and Performances

During the holiday season, Broadway lights up with a variety of festive shows, allowing visitors to enjoy world-class theatre while immersed in holiday cheer. One of the most popular productions is "A Christmas Carol," the classic Dickens story about Ebenezer Scrooge's transformation from a miser to a man full of Christmas spirit. The 2024 adaptation will be staged at the Lyceum Theatre, 149 W 45th St, from November 22 to January 3, 2025. This version of "A Christmas Carol" is known for its stunning sets and moving performances, making it an ideal holiday outing for families or anyone looking for a story rich in tradition and heart.

Ticket prices for "A Christmas Carol" typically range from $49 to $189, with the best seats selling out quickly, especially for weekend and evening performances. Booking early through Broadway.com or Telecharge is strongly advised. Weekday matinees are an excellent option for those on a tight budget, as they provide not only a less crowded theatre but also lower ticket prices. Furthermore, "The Nutcracker" by the New York City Ballet, while not technically a Broadway show, is a Christmas tradition. This magical ballet, held at the David H. Koch Theater at Lincoln Center, 10 Lincoln Center Plaza, from November 24, 2024, to December 31, 2024, brings Tchaikovsky's enchanting score to life with toy soldiers, dancing snowflakes, and the famous Sugar Plum Fairy.

If you want to see "The Nutcracker," expect ticket prices to start around $45, with premium seats going up to $285 on the most popular dates. Tickets are available through the New York City Ballet website, and it is recommended that you book early, especially for high-demand performances on Christmas Eve and Christmas Day.

Holiday concerts at Carnegie Hall and Lincoln Center.

Carnegie Hall and Lincoln Center are popular venues for holiday concerts and world-class performances. Carnegie Hall, located at 881 7th Ave, hosts a series of holiday-themed concerts throughout December. One of the most anticipated events is the New York String Orchestra's annual Christmas Eve concert, a lovely celebration of classical music that has become a beloved holiday tradition. Throughout the month, you can also see a variety of performances, including renowned choirs singing holiday carols and orchestras playing beloved seasonal pieces like Handel's "Messiah."

Ticket prices at Carnegie Hall vary by performance, ranging from $20 to $150. The Christmas Eve concert typically starts at $49, with premium seats available for a higher price. It's a good idea to purchase tickets in advance, especially for popular performances, either through the Carnegie Hall website or at the box office.

In addition to "The Nutcracker," Lincoln Center offers festive performances by the New York Philharmonic. Held at David Geffen Hall, these concerts bring classic holiday music to life, making them an excellent choice for those looking to combine the beauty of symphonic music with the warmth of the holiday season. Prices for these concerts range between $40 and $160, depending on the performance and seating. The Lincoln Center website allows you to book online, and students and seniors may be eligible for discounts on select performances.

Holiday Parades and Outdoor Events

No holiday trip to New York is complete without attending one of the city's grand outdoor events. The Macy's Thanksgiving Day Parade, held every year on Thanksgiving morning, signals the unofficial start of the Christmas season in New York. The 2024 parade will, as always, feature iconic giant balloons, impressive floats, and live performances, culminating with Santa Claus' arrival. The parade begins at 77th Street and Central Park West and travels down to 34th Street, passing by Macy's Herald Square.

While the parade is free to attend, prime viewing areas fill up quickly. If you want a good view, arrive early—by 6 a.m.—to secure a spot along the route. Alternatively, many hotels along the parade route provide special packages that include a room with a view of the parade, allowing you to watch the spectacle in comfort. If you want to avoid the crowds, consider attending Inflation Eve, which takes place the night before the parade at 79th Street and Columbus Avenue, where you can watch massive balloons being inflated in preparation for the big day.

For those seeking a more intimate holiday experience, the annual Washington Square Park Christmas Tree Lighting is a charming tradition. This year's lighting will be held under the iconic arch at 5th Avenue and Waverly Place on December 4, 2024, at 5 p.m. The event includes carolling, holiday lights, and a visit from Santa Claus, all in the historic and charming setting of Greenwich Village. It's a free event and an excellent opportunity to see how a local community celebrates Christmas away from the crowds of Midtown.

The New York Botanical Garden's Holiday Train Show

The Holiday Train Show at the New York Botanical Garden is a must-see for families and those looking for a one-of-a-kind holiday experience. This enchanting display, located at the New York Botanical Garden at 2900 Southern Blvd in The Bronx, features model trains travelling through miniature replicas of New York's most famous landmarks, all made from natural materials such as bark, leaves, and twigs. The 2024 edition of the train show will run from November 18, 2024, to January 21, 2025, giving you plenty of time to attend.

Adult tickets start at $35 on weekdays and $39 on weekends, while children's tickets (ages 2 to 12) cost between $18 and $23. Tickets can be purchased on the New York Botanical Garden website, and reservations are strongly advised, especially on weekends and holidays when the event is particularly popular. If you want a more festive, grown-up experience, go to Bar Car Nights, a special after-hours event that includes seasonal cocktails, live entertainment, and a tour of the holiday displays. Tickets for Bar Car Nights begin at $55, making it an enjoyable way to celebrate the holiday season in a more relaxed, adult environment.

A Festive Season of Entertainment.

New York City in 2024 promises a diverse and stunning array of holiday entertainment, with something for everyone. Whether you're captivated by the grandeur of the Radio City Christmas Spectacular, moved by the timeless elegance of a Carnegie Hall concert, or enchanted by the whimsical charm of the Holiday Train Show, the city will provide you with unforgettable holiday memories. With so many events to choose from, it's critical to plan ahead of time, purchase tickets in advance, and take advantage of the unique experiences that only New York can provide during the holiday season. In the following chapter, we'll walk you through the city's best outdoor winter experiences, including top ice skating rinks and picturesque snowy spots for a holiday stroll.

NYC's Winter Wonderlands

As winter descends upon New York City, the entire landscape transforms into a picturesque wonderland, ideal for outdoor activities that celebrate the holiday spirit. From gliding across ice rinks beneath iconic landmarks to strolls through snow-dusted parks, the city provides numerous opportunities to appreciate the season's natural beauty. In this chapter, we'll walk you through the best winter experiences New York has to offer, whether you're an experienced skater, a family looking for outdoor fun, or a visitor looking for a peaceful winter getaway.

Ice Skating at Rockefeller Center: A New York Classic.

Few things are more "New York at Christmas" than skating beneath the towering tree at Rockefeller Center, located at 45 Rockefeller Plaza, New York, NY 10111. With the twinkling lights of the Christmas tree overhead and the bustling heart of Midtown surrounding you, this rink is perhaps the city's most iconic skating destination. It is open from November 2024 to early January 2025, and the experience of gliding on the ice is nothing short of magical.

Skating at The Rink at Rockefeller Center is one of the most popular holiday activities, so expect crowds, particularly on weekends and close to Christmas. To ensure a spot, book your skating session in advance through the Rockefeller Center website, as time slots tend to sell out quickly. Skating tickets cost $21 to $58, depending on the time of day and season, with higher prices during peak holiday periods. Skate rentals are available for an additional $15, and lockers are available to store your belongings while on the ice. VIP packages are available for those looking for a more elevated experience, including exclusive rink access and complimentary hot chocolate.

Bryant Park Winter Village offers free skating and holiday shopping.

Bryant Park's Winter Village, located a short walk from Times Square, offers a winter wonderland in the heart of Midtown. This popular destination, located at 6th Avenue and 42nd Street in New York, NY 10018, combines holiday shopping with free ice skating. The Bank of America Winter Village Rink is New York's only free-admission ice skating rink, making it an excellent choice for budget-conscious visitors seeking to enjoy the season's outdoor activities.

The rink will be open from late October 2024 to early March 2025, giving you plenty of time to enjoy skating under the New York City skyline. While skating admission is free, skate rentals range from $25 to $45, depending on the date, so if you bring your skates, you can enjoy the rink for free. Children and beginners can also use a variety of skate aids. After skating, you can explore the nearby holiday shops, which feature over 170 custom-designed kiosks selling a variety of gifts, artisanal products, and seasonal treats. From cosy wool scarves to handcrafted ornaments, the Winter Village is the ideal place to pick up last-minute holiday gifts or do some festive shopping.

If skating isn't your thing, Bryant Park also has a variety of food vendors serving everything from warm hot chocolate to Belgian waffles, giving you plenty of options for warming up after a cold session on the ice.

Central Park: Snowy Strolls and Iconic Ice Rinks

Nothing captures the essence of winter in New York quite like a snowy stroll through Central Park, especially when the city's iconic park is blanketed in white. The park's expansive pathways, bridges, and quiet corners provide a peaceful respite from the holiday hustle. The Mall, with its stately elm trees lining the pathway, is especially beautiful in the winter, when snow accumulates on the branches, creating a magical setting for a winter walk. Another favourite is the iconic Bow Bridge, which provides breathtaking views of the snow-covered park and the Ramble, making it an ideal location for photography or a quiet moment of reflection.

Wollman Rink, located at 830 5th Ave., New York, NY 10065, offers an enchanting skating experience with the city skyline as a backdrop. Wollman Rink, open from late October to March, is larger than many of the city's other rinks, providing more space to skate in the heart of Central Park. Adult admission ranges from $12 to $23 depending on the day of the week, with skate rentals available for an additional $11. Lasker Rink, located on the park's northern end, provides a more local, low-key atmosphere, making it ideal for families or those looking for a quieter skate.

After your time on the ice, Central Park has countless picturesque spots to explore. The Bethesda Terrace and Fountain are especially beautiful in the snow, and for those feeling adventurous, the park's hilly terrain near Great Hill and Pilgrim Hill is ideal for sledging when it snows heavily.

The Rink at Brookfield Place: Skating With a View of the Hudson

The Rink at Brookfield Place, located at 230 Vesey St, New York, NY 10281 in Lower Manhattan, offers a more contemporary skating experience with stunning views of the Hudson River. This rink, open from late November to mid-March, provides a sleek, sophisticated alternative to the more tourist-heavy locations. Skating here feels quieter and more upscale, thanks to the scenic waterfront setting and proximity to high-end shopping and dining.

Admission to The Rink at Brookfield Place costs $17, with skate rentals available for an additional $5. The rink provides skating lessons, including small group sessions and private lessons, making it an excellent choice for beginners or those looking to improve their technique. After your time on the ice, you can relax with a hot drink at one of the nearby cafés or browse the luxury shops in

Brookfield Place, which include high-end retailers and gourmet food halls.

Sledding in New York City: Top Spots for Snowy Fun

While ice skating is a popular winter activity for many, sledging provides a nostalgic and thrilling way to enjoy the snow in New York City. When the snowfall is just right, several of the city's parks become popular sledging areas, allowing both locals and visitors to enjoy some snowy fun. Pilgrim Hill in Central Park, near 72nd Street and 5th Avenue, is known for its steep incline and smooth runs, making it one of the city's best sledging spots. On snowy weekends, the hill is packed with families and children racing down the slopes on brightly coloured sledges.

For a quieter sledging experience, visit Riverside Park on the Upper West Side, where the gentle hills near 91st Street make an ideal backdrop for casual sledging. Another favourite is Prospect Park in Brooklyn, where Long Meadow Hill provides ample space for sledders of all ages to enjoy the snowy landscape.

For those who do not own a sledge, many local stores in the surrounding areas sell them during the winter season, and you can check local rental shops for availability. Sledging in New York is a simple pleasure, ideal for anyone looking to enjoy the winter weather in a fun and active manner.

Embracing Winter in NYC's Outdoor Spaces

Winter in New York City brings a variety of activities that allow both visitors and locals to enjoy the season's beauty and festive atmosphere. Whether you're skating beneath the sparkling lights at Rockefeller Center, strolling through a snow-covered Central Park, or sledging down one of the city's many hills, there are numerous ways to experience the magic of New York's winter wonderland.

Each rink, park, and open space has its distinct take on the season, ensuring that there is something for everyone to enjoy, regardless of the weather. In the following chapter, we'll look at New York's festive dining options and highlight the best places to eat holiday meals and seasonal treats across the city.

Holiday Dining and Festive Treats

New York City's culinary scene shines brightly during the holiday season. From lavish Christmas dinners at fine dining establishments to cosy cafés serving seasonal treats, there is no shortage of delectable holiday fare to sample. Whether you're looking for a lavish feast on Christmas Eve, a warm cup of hot chocolate after a day of skating, or unique seasonal bites at the city's famous holiday markets, New York's restaurants and cafés have something for everyone. In this chapter, we'll look at the best holiday dining experiences, from traditional Christmas dinners to the most sought-after seasonal sweets, to make your time in New York City as enjoyable for your taste buds as it is for your eyes.

Where to Enjoy a Classic Christmas Dinner in New York City

Many of New York City's finest restaurants offer special holiday menus that capture the essence of the season, allowing you to enjoy a traditional Christmas meal with all the trimmings. *The Plaza Hotel*, located at 768 5th Ave, New York, NY 10019, is a well-known destination for a luxurious holiday meal. The Palm Court, located within the hotel, is well-known for its Christmas Eve and Christmas Day dining experiences, where guests can enjoy a festive, multi-course meal amidst elegant décor. Expect beautifully roasted meats, classic sides like chestnut stuffing, and festive desserts like gingerbread and peppermint. Reservations for The Palm Court's holiday dining are required and should be made well in advance, as it is one of the city's most popular dining options around Christmas.

For a more modern take on the holiday feast, visit The *River Café in Brooklyn*, located at 1 Water St, Brooklyn, NY 11201. The River Café, which boasts stunning views of the Manhattan skyline and the Brooklyn Bridge, serves a special Christmas menu featuring seasonal seafood, farm-to-table ingredients, and an award-winning wine list. Dining here provides an intimate and upscale experience, ideal for couples or small groups looking to celebrate in style. Christmas Eve and Christmas Day menus frequently feature dishes like lobster bisque, roasted duck, and decadent chocolate desserts, all presented with a festive flair.

If you want something more cosy and homey, *Freemans*, located at the end of an alley at Freeman Alley, New York, NY 10002, provides a rustic, warm environment with hearty holiday meals that are ideal for those seeking a more relaxed atmosphere. Their Christmas Eve menu usually includes comforting dishes such as roasted pork loin, savoury pies, and rich bread pudding. With its candle-lit interior and antique décor, Freemans feels like a hidden gem in the heart of the city, providing the ideal escape from the holiday rush.

Family-Friendly Holiday Dining

Carmine's on Broadway, located at 200 W 44th St, New York, NY 10036, is a classic Italian restaurant that goes all out for Christmas. Carmine's, known for its large, family-style portions, serves a festive menu featuring Italian-American favourites such as baked ziti, spaghetti and meatballs, and tiramisu. Their grand Christmas décor, complete with twinkling lights and garlands, makes it an inviting spot for families looking to share a hearty meal after a day exploring the city's holiday attractions.

Tavern on the Green, located at 67th Street & Central Park West, New York, NY 10023, is another excellent family dining option. This iconic restaurant, nestled within Central Park, is decked out in sparkling holiday lights during the Christmas season and offers both indoor and outdoor seating (including heated areas for those chilly winter nights). The menu includes holiday favourites such as roasted turkey, honey-glazed ham, and warm apple pie, making it an ideal spot for families looking to eat after a winter walk through Central Park or a skate at Wollman Rink.

Holiday Sweets and Treats: Must-Try Seasonal Delights

New York City is known for its incredible dessert scene, and during the holidays, bakeries and cafés throughout the city offer seasonal sweets that capture the flavours of Christmas. *Dominique Ansel Bakery's* "Christmas Morning Cereal," a limited-edition creation with caramelized hazelnuts, chocolate puffs, and smoked cinnamon meringues, is a well-known holiday treat. The bakery, located at 189 Spring St, New York, NY 10012, also serves its famous hot chocolate, which is topped with a blossoming marshmallow flower that unfolds in your cup, creating a delightful Instagram-worthy moment as well as a tasty treat.

Bouchon Bakery at 10 Columbus Circle, New York, NY 10019 offers traditional French holiday pastries like bûche de Noël (yule log) and panettone. The bakery's warm and cosy interior, combined with its stunning holiday-themed pastries, make it the ideal place to grab a sweet treat between shopping trips or before a holiday performance at nearby Lincoln Center.

No Christmas in New York is complete without visiting one of the city's many holiday markets, where you can find a variety of seasonal snacks and treats. Spiced cider, roasted chestnuts, and German-inspired gingerbread cookies will keep you warm at the Union Square Holiday Market and Bryant Park Winter Village. These markets also feature gourmet food stalls selling everything from artisanal chocolates to freshly baked pastries, making them ideal for grabbing a quick festive bite while shopping for holiday gifts.

Hot Chocolate and Cozy Winter Cafes

Nothing beats warming up with a cup of hot chocolate after a long day of sightseeing or holiday shopping. City Bakery, located at 3 W 18th St, New York, NY 10011, serves some of the city's best hot chocolates. Their hot chocolate is legendary for its thick, almost pudding-like consistency and comes with a large homemade marshmallow. Each cup is a decadent treat, ideal for sipping while admiring Manhattan's wintry streets.

For a more European-style hot chocolate experience, visit **L.A. Burdick** at 5 E 20th St, New York, NY 10003, where you can sample a variety of hot chocolates made from single-origin dark chocolates and served in elegant little cups. Their café is a warm, inviting space where you can relax and enjoy your drink while sampling a variety of house-made truffles and bonbons, all beautifully decorated for the holidays.

If you find yourself near Greenwich Village, stop by **Café Dante** at 79-81 Macdougal St, New York, NY 10012 for a cosy, intimate experience. Café Dante is well-known for its signature cocktails and delicious espresso drinks, but it also serves a festive hot chocolate spiced with winter flavours such as cinnamon and nutmeg. Their welcoming atmosphere makes it the ideal place to unwind after a day of exploring the city's tourist attractions.

Festive Food at NYC's Holiday Markets

New York's holiday markets are not only a great place to find unique gifts, but they're also a foodie's dream, with a wide variety of seasonal snacks and festive street food. At Bryant Park's Winter Village and Union Square Holiday Market, you can eat everything from Belgian waffles and crêpes to bratwurst and pierogi. These markets are the perfect place to grab a quick bite while taking in the festive atmosphere. Hot cider, mulled wine, and spiced doughnuts are also popular during the colder months, providing a sweet way to keep warm while browsing the market stalls.

If you're looking for something a little more substantial, go to The Pennsy, a food hall located just steps from **Penn Station** at 2 Pennsylvania Plaza, New York, NY 10121. You'll find a variety of gourmet vendors selling everything from lobster rolls to sushi. Many of the stalls offer holiday specials, such as holiday-themed sandwiches, soups, and desserts. It's an excellent choice for those looking for a quick but high-quality bite in between touring the city's Christmas lights and attractions.

Christmas in New York City is about more than just the festive sights; it's also about indulging in some of the city's best cuisine. Whether you're having a grand Christmas dinner at one of the city's fine dining establishments, sampling sweet treats at a holiday market, or snuggling up with a rich cup of hot chocolate, New York's holiday dining scene is filled with warmth and wonder. The diverse range of options, from luxurious meals to casual street food, ensures that every visitor finds something to satisfy their holiday cravings. In the following chapter, we'll look at the best places to buy unique Christmas gifts, from upscale boutiques to festive holiday markets.

Where to Stay in NYC for Christmas.

When it comes to finding a place to stay in New York City during the Christmas season, the city has a variety of options for every type of traveller. Whether you're looking for a luxurious holiday escape, a cosy boutique experience, or a family-friendly hotel with festive activities, New York's hotels celebrate the holiday season with special decorations, events, and services that will make your stay unforgettable. In this chapter, we'll look at the best places to stay during the holiday season to help you find the ideal home base for your Christmas adventure in New York City.

7.1 Luxury Festive Hotels

For those looking for the ultimate luxury experience, New York's top hotels provide an unforgettable holiday atmosphere. *The Plaza Hotel*, located at 768 5th Ave, New York, NY 10019, is one of the most iconic places to stay during the Christmas season. The Plaza, known for its glamorous décor and long history as a symbol of New York luxury, is a popular holiday destination. During the holidays, the hotel's public areas are transformed with twinkling lights, grand Christmas trees, and elaborate floral arrangements. The Palm Court is particularly well-known for its elegant holiday afternoon tea, where guests can savour festive treats like gingerbread and scones in the hotel's opulent setting. For those seeking a true New

35

York holiday experience, The Plaza even offers a "Home Alone 2" package, which commemorates the iconic film shot at the hotel. Rooms at The Plaza during the holiday season typically start around $1,000 per night, but reservations are required because the hotel is in high demand at this time.

The Peninsula New York, located at 700 5th Avenue, New York, NY 10019, is another excellent option for luxurious Christmas accommodations. This elegant hotel is well-known for its festive decorations, which include an elaborate Christmas tree and holiday lights on the building's grand façade. The Peninsula offers a variety of holiday packages, including festive afternoon teas, holiday-themed spa treatments, and in-room Christmas tree decorating services. After a day of exploring the city's Christmas attractions, guests can relax at the hotel's Peninsula Spa, which offers treatments infused with seasonal scents such as cinnamon and pine. The Peninsula's rates start around $900 per night during the holidays, making it an ideal destination for travellers looking for luxury and relaxation.

The Langham, New York, located at 400 5th Ave., New York, NY 10018, offers a more intimate luxury experience. This contemporary hotel has stunning views of the Empire State Building and is known for its understated elegance. The Langham celebrates the festive season with tasteful decorations and special dining events, such as holiday brunches at the hotel's Michelin-starred restaurant, Ai Fiori. With its quiet yet central location,

The Langham is ideal for those who want to enjoy the city's holiday attractions while relaxing in a serene and sophisticated setting. During the Christmas season, room rates typically start at $700 per night.

7.2 Cozy Boutique Hotels with Holiday Charm.

For travellers looking for a more intimate and unique experience, New York's boutique hotels provide plenty of holiday charm without the grand scale of the city's luxury giants. One notable establishment is *The NoMad Hotel*, located at 1170 Broadway, New York, NY 10001. This boutique hotel is housed in a beautifully restored Beaux-Arts building and offers a mix of traditional New York elegance and contemporary luxury. The NoMad celebrates the holiday season with cosy, warm décor and a special holiday menu at The NoMad Restaurant, featuring seasonal dishes such as roasted duck and chestnut soup. The hotel's dark wood interiors and plush furnishings create a welcoming, stylish atmosphere after a day of holiday shopping or sightseeing. Rooms at The NoMad start around $450 per night in December.

For those seeking a more eclectic and artistic atmosphere, *The High Line Hotel* in Chelsea is an excellent choice. This boutique hotel, located at 180 10th Avenue, New York, NY 10011, is housed in a former seminary and has a charming, historic ambience that feels especially magical during the holiday season. The High Line Hotel is well-known for its holiday decorations, which include twinkling lights, wreaths, and a cosy lobby café where guests can warm up with hot chocolate or a festive cocktail. The hotel's unique blend of Gothic architecture and modern touches creates a tranquil oasis just steps away from the bustling Chelsea Market and the High Line Park. The High Line Hotel's rooms typically start at $350 per night during the holiday season.

Another charming option is *The Marlton Hotel*, which can be found at 5 W 8th St, New York, NY 10011. This Greenwich Village gem has a cosy, European-inspired atmosphere that is ideal for those seeking a more intimate and personal vacation experience. The Marlton's vintage-inspired décor, which includes dark wood panelling, Persian rugs, and a roaring fireplace in the lobby, creates a warm and inviting space to escape the winter chill. Margaux, the hotel's in-house restaurant, serves a delicious seasonal menu that includes winter cocktails and hearty dishes such as roast chicken and squash risotto. With room rates starting around $300 per night, The Marlton is an affordable yet stylish choice for vacationers.

7.3 Family-Friendly Accommodations with Christmas Activities

Families visiting New York during the holidays will find a variety of hotels that cater to both adults and children, with special holiday activities and amenities to make the season even more magical. The *Ritz-Carlton* New York, Central Park, located at 50 Central Park South, New York, NY 10019, is an excellent choice for families. With its prime location next to Central Park, the hotel provides convenient access to family-friendly holiday activities such as ice skating at Wollman Rink and carriage rides through the park. The Ritz-Carlton goes all out for holiday decorations, transforming the lobby into a winter wonderland complete with a grand Christmas tree and festive lights. The hotel has a special Ritz Kids Program that includes holiday-themed crafts, cookie decorating, and even an in-room visit from Santa Claus on Christmas Eve. The Ritz-Carlton's holiday room rates begin at $1,200 per night.

For families seeking a more affordable option, The *Residence Inn by Marriott* Times Square at 1033 Avenue of the Americas, New York, NY 10018, provides spacious suites with kitchenettes, ideal for families who want to prepare meals or snacks. The hotel is a short walk from Bryant Park and its Winter Village, making it convenient to visit the holiday markets and go ice skating. The Residence Inn also provides free breakfast, which is ideal for families getting an early start on their Christmas adventures. During the holiday season, rooms here start around $400 per night, making it an affordable option without sacrificing comfort or location.

Lotte New York Palace, located at 455 Madison Avenue, New York, NY 10022, is another excellent family option. This grand hotel is well-known for its stunning holiday decorations, which include a massive Christmas tree in the courtyard, making for ideal family photo opportunities. Lotte New York Palace provides special holiday packages that include in-room stockings for children, a family movie night featuring Christmas classics, and even private ice skating lessons at Rockefeller Center. With room rates starting at $600 per night, this family-friendly hotel combines luxury with festive fun, ensuring that both children and parents have an unforgettable Christmas experience.

Finding Your Ideal Holiday Stay

New York City has a wide range of accommodations that capture the festive spirit of Christmas, from luxurious hotels with grand holiday displays to cosy boutique stays full of charm. Whether you're travelling as a couple, with family, or on your own, there's a great place to stay that will make your trip to the city even more enjoyable.

From the opulence of The Plaza and The Peninsula to the intimate warmth of The Marlton Hotel, New York's hotels provide more than just a place to sleep, but also a place to make lasting vacation memories. In the following chapter, we'll look at the best places to shop for unique Christmas gifts, from high-end boutiques to festive holiday markets, so you can return home with treasures as memorable as your trip.

Looking for the Best NYC Christmas Souvenirs

New York City is a shopper's dream all year, but during the Christmas season, it transforms into a festive wonderland, making it one of the best places in the world to find unique gifts and holiday souvenirs. From luxury boutiques on Fifth Avenue to quaint speciality stores and iconic department stores decked out in holiday splendour, there are plenty of places to find the perfect gift for loved ones—or yourself. In this chapter, we'll show you the most magical shopping spots in New York, each with its own unique holiday experience.

8.1 Fifth Avenue: Luxury Shopping in a Festive Wonderland.

Nothing beats *Fifth Avenue* for holiday shopping. This iconic shopping district, which stretches from 49th to 60th Streets, is lined with luxury department stores and high-end boutiques that are all lavishly decorated for the holiday season. The window displays on Fifth Avenue are an attraction in and of themselves, attracting crowds of visitors eager to see the elaborate and imaginative designs.

Saks Fifth Avenue, located at 611 5th Ave, New York, NY 10022, is a must-see holiday destination. Saks is well-known for its legendary light show, which illuminates the store's façade every night throughout the season. It also has some of the most spectacular holiday window displays in the city. Inside, you'll find a dazzling array of designer brands, including Chanel, Gucci, Prada, and Saint Laurent, making it ideal for high-end gift shopping. In December, the store also sells exclusive holiday collections and limited-edition items that make ideal one-of-a-kind gifts.

Bergdorf Goodman, located at 754 Fifth Avenue, New York, NY 10019, is another luxury shopping landmark. Bergdorf is famous for its elaborate holiday window displays, which can take months to create and feature intricate scenes that combine fashion, art, and storytelling. Inside the store, you'll find the best in luxury fashion, fine jewellery, and exclusive accessories, ideal for those looking to splurge on something special this Christmas.

If you want something more personal, visit *Tiffany & Co*. at 727 5th Avenue, New York, NY 10022. Tiffany's, known for its elegant jewellery, also sells beautiful holiday décor and collectable ornaments, all packaged in the brand's signature blue box. A visit to this iconic jeweller during the holiday season feels like stepping into a holiday fairytale, and you're sure to find a meaningful gift that will be treasured.

8.2 Top Boutiques for Unique Christmas Gifts

While Fifth Avenue is synonymous with luxury, New York City is also home to a plethora of smaller boutiques where you can find more unique and personal gifts. SoHo boasts an eclectic mix of independent stores, designer shops, and artistic boutiques selling everything from handcrafted jewellery to quirky home décor.

One standout is Clic, which can be found at 255 Centre St, New York, NY 10013. This chic boutique sells a carefully curated selection of art, photography books, home goods, and fashion accessories. During the holiday season, Clic offers beautifully designed stationery, one-of-a-kind art prints, and handcrafted ornaments, making it the ideal place to find creative and artistic gifts.

If you're looking for eco-friendly and sustainable gifts, *Package Free* at 116 N 11th St, Brooklyn, NY 11249 is a must-stop. This environmentally conscious store sells a variety of zero-waste products such as reusable straws, beeswax wraps, and sustainable beauty products. Their holiday collection frequently includes stylish gift sets that are both practical and eco-friendly, making them ideal for the environmentally-conscious person on your list.

For something truly one-of-a-kind, visit *ABC Carpet & Home*, located at 888 Broadway, New York, NY 10003. This massive store is stocked with luxurious home décor items, artisan-crafted furniture, and textiles sourced from all over the world. ABC Carpet & Home transforms into a winter wonderland during the holidays, with a wide selection of festive decorations, ornaments, and handcrafted gifts. This store is a treasure trove of one-of-a-kind finds, whether it's a hand-embroidered pillow or a stunning piece of jewellery.

8.3 Specialty Stores: FAO Schwarz, Macy's Santaland, and more.

During the holiday season, New York's famous speciality stores are a must-see for those seeking nostalgia and childlike wonder. *FAO Schwarz*, located at 30 Rockefeller Plaza, New York, NY 10111, is one of the world's most iconic toy stores, and it becomes even more magical during the Christmas season. FAO Schwarz, known for its giant piano (made famous in the film "Big") and life-size stuffed animals, sells a wide range of toys, games, and collectables for both children and adults. The store's holiday decorations are a sight to behold, and you're sure to find something fun and whimsical for the children on your list—or those who are simply young at heart.

Macy's Herald Square, located at 151 West 34th Street, New York, NY 10001, is another holiday staple. Macy's is well-known for its incredible selection of clothing, accessories, and housewares, as well as its legendary Santaland. Every year, Macy's transforms a section of its eighth floor into a winter wonderland, complete with twinkling lights, animatronic reindeer, and a visit from Santa Claus himself. Visiting Santaland is a beloved family tradition, and it's the ideal place to get Christmas ornaments, festive home décor, or personalized gifts. If you're visiting Macy's during the holidays, make sure to reserve a timed entry to Santaland in advance, as it's a popular attraction.

Eataly, located at 200 5th Ave, New York, NY 10010, offers a diverse selection of gourmet Italian products, making it an excellent location for holiday shopping. Eataly's festive selection includes everything from artisanal pasta and olive oil to beautifully wrapped panettone and chocolates, making it ideal for putting together an Italian-themed gift basket or simply indulging in seasonal treats. During December, Eataly also hosts special holiday markets with handmade products from Italian artisans, adding a cultural touch to your Christmas shopping.

New York's Christmas Shopping Wonderland.

Whether you're browsing Fifth Avenue's luxury stores, exploring SoHo's boutique shops, or reliving childhood memories at FAO Schwarz, New York City has an endless supply of perfect Christmas gifts and souvenirs. Each shopping destination offers a distinct experience, from the gleaming window displays of department stores to the hidden treasures of independent boutiques. Whether you want to splurge on a high-end item or find something unique, New York's holiday shopping scene has something for everyone. In the following chapter, we'll look at practical tips for navigating the city during the busy Christmas season, so your holiday trip runs smoothly from beginning to end.

Cultural Christmas Traditions in New York City

New York City is a cultural melting pot, and during the holiday season, the city's many traditions and celebrations reflect this diversity beautifully. From attending religious services at iconic churches to participating in tree lighting ceremonies and experiencing the multicultural vibrancy of Hanukkah and Kwanzaa, Christmas in New York is about more than just lights and presents—it's about the rich traditions that bring people together. In this chapter, we'll look at some of the city's most beloved cultural and holiday traditions, giving visitors a better understanding of how New York celebrates the holiday season.

9.1 Attending the Midnight Mass at St. Patrick's Cathedral

For many people, attending Midnight Mass on Christmas Eve is one of the most sacred and meaningful holiday traditions. No venue in New York City is more awe-inspiring for this tradition than St. Patrick's Cathedral, located on 5th Avenue between 50th and 51st Streets, New York, NY 10022. This breathtaking neo-Gothic cathedral is the largest Catholic church in the United States and an architectural marvel that draws visitors from all over the world.

The Midnight Mass at St. Patrick's Cathedral is a deeply spiritual event, marked by solemnity and reverence, accompanied by the choir's angelic voices, the sound of the grand organ, and the glow of candles. This service, hosted by the Archbishop of New York, is a major event on the city's Christmas calendar, attracting both locals and tourists. The mass begins at midnight on December 24, but you must arrive early because the cathedral fills up quickly, with doors opening around 10 p.m. Those who are unable to attend in person can usually watch a live stream of the mass, making it available to worshippers all over the world.

If you plan on attending, dress warmly and be prepared to wait, as seating is first-come, first-served. The cathedral's grandeur and the solemnity of the occasion make the effort worthwhile. Midnight Mass at St. Patrick's provides a powerful opportunity to reflect on the true meaning of Christmas in one of the city's most iconic settings.

9.2 Christmas Tree Lighting Ceremonies Throughout the City

New York City is famous for its extravagant Christmas trees, and the lighting ceremonies that kick off the holiday season are popular among both locals and visitors. Perhaps the most well-known of these is the *Rockefeller Center* Christmas Tree Lighting, which takes place every year at 45 Rockefeller Plaza, New York, NY 10111. This grand event, which usually takes place in late November or early December, attracts thousands of people to Rockefeller Plaza and millions more who watch on television. The lighting of the towering tree, adorned with tens of thousands of LED lights and topped with the iconic Swarovski crystal star, is accompanied by live performances from well-known musicians and choirs, making it one of the city's most popular holiday events.

While the Rockefeller Center tree may be the most famous, numerous other tree lighting ceremonies throughout the city provide an aree-light-in intimate or local experience. *Bryant Park* hosts its own tree lighting ceremony at 6th Avenue and 42nd Street, usually in early December. The park's tree lighting is part of the Winter Village festivities, which also include live entertainment, free ice skating, and visits from Santa Claus. This family-friendly event provides a more relaxed alternative to Rockefeller's crowds while retaining holiday magic.

Another popular holiday tradition is the annual Christmas Tree Lighting Ceremony in *Washington Square Park*, which is located at 5th Avenue and Waverly Place. The ceremony, which takes place beneath the park's famous arch, features carolling, festive lights, and a visit from Santa, making for a cosy, community-driven experience. The lighting usually takes place in early December, with a second evening of carolling planned closer to Christmas Eve. The tree itself, beautifully framed by the iconic arch, is a breathtaking sight, especially against the backdrop of Lower Manhattan.

Regardless of where you go to see a tree lighting in New York, these events are a heartwarming way to celebrate the season and capture the communal spirit that defines Christmas in the city.

9.3 Celebrating Various Holiday Traditions: Hanukkah and Kwanzaa in NYC

In addition to Christmas, New York City proudly embraces its rich cultural and religious diversity during the holiday season, with lively celebrations of Hanukkah and Kwanzaa. The city's large Jewish community celebrates Hanukkah, the Festival of Lights, with menorah lightings, festive events, and cultural performances throughout the five boroughs.

The *lighting of the World's Largest Menorah* at Grand Army Plaza in Manhattan, across from Central Park and the iconic Plaza Hotel, is one of the city's most well-known Hanukkah events. This massive menorah stands 32 feet tall and is lit every night of Hanukkah, beginning at 5:30 p.m. (earlier times on Fridays to accommodate the Sabbath). The event features live music, hot latkes, and a variety of family-friendly activities, making it a joyful and lively celebration open to people from all backgrounds. Another large menorah is lit at Grand Army Plaza in Brooklyn, near Prospect Park, where similar festivities occur each night of Hanukkah.

For those seeking a deeper cultural connection, The *Jewish Museum*, located at 1109 5th Ave, New York, NY 10128, hosts several Hanukkah-themed exhibits and programs throughout the season. The museum frequently hosts special events, such as art workshops and storytelling for children, making it an excellent educational experience for families over the holidays.

Kwanzaa, which celebrates African-American culture and heritage, is also an important part of New York's holiday celebrations. The city hosts numerous Kwanzaa events that reflect the holiday's principles of unity, self-determination, and collective responsibility through music, dance, and cultural performance. The Apollo Theater, located at 253 W 125th St, New York, NY 10027, hosts one of the largest Kwanzaa celebrations in Harlem. The Apollo's annual Kwanzaa celebration includes traditional African dance, live music, spoken word performances, and workshops emphasizing the holiday's cultural significance. It's a lively, community-oriented event that celebrates African-American culture while inviting people from all backgrounds to join in the fun.

Another significant Kwanzaa celebration is held at the American Museum of Natural History, located at 200 Central Park West, New York, NY 10024. Every year, the museum hosts a Kwanzaa Festival, which includes performances, craft workshops, and a marketplace where visitors can buy handcrafted items from African-American artisans. This family-friendly event teaches about Kwanzaa's history and significance while celebrating the diversity of African culture.

Accepting the Spirit of New York's Cultural Traditions.

Christmas in New York City is about more than just lights and decorations; it's about honouring the city's incredible cultural diversity and the traditions that bring its people together. Whether you're attending Midnight Mass at St. Patrick's Cathedral, watching one of the many tree-lighting ceremonies, or participating in the vibrant celebrations of Hanukkah and Kwanzaa, the holiday season in New York has something for everyone.

These traditions, which are rooted in faith, culture, and community, highlight the true meaning of the season: coming together to celebrate love, joy, and common humanity. In the following chapter, we'll offer practical tips and advice for navigating the city during the busy holiday season, ensuring that your trip runs as smoothly and enjoyable as possible.

Recommended Itineraries for NYC Christmas

New York City is a magical destination during the holiday season, and with so many festive sights and activities, it can be difficult to decide what to prioritize. Whether you're a first-time visitor, travelling with family, or looking for a romantic holiday getaway, these carefully curated itineraries will help you make the most of your Christmas in the Big Apple. Each itinerary focuses on key experiences, providing the ideal balance of iconic attractions and seasonal events to ensure you make unforgettable memories.

10.1 Three-Day Itinerary for First-Time Visitors: Must-See Vacation Destinations

If this is your first time visiting New York during the holidays, you'll want to see the city's most famous attractions while enjoying the festive atmosphere. This three-day itinerary includes iconic landmarks, holiday markets, and must-see events to make your Christmas trip truly memorable.

Day one: Rockefeller Center, Fifth Avenue, and Radio City. Begin your Christmas adventure at Rockefeller Center. Arrive early to avoid crowds and see the famous Rockefeller Center Christmas Tree in its full glory at 45 Rockefeller Plaza. After admiring the towering tree, head to the Rockefeller Rink and ice skate under the twinkling lights. Make sure to reserve your skate session in advance, as this is one of the most popular holiday activities.

After skating, stroll down Fifth Avenue to see the stunning holiday window displays at Saks Fifth Avenue, Bergdorf Goodman, and other luxury stores. The creative window designs are a holiday tradition, with each year bringing something new and magical to see.

In the evening, take in the Radio City Christmas Spectacular at Radio City Music Hall (1260 6th Ave), where you'll be treated to an incredible show featuring the world-renowned Rockettes. This high-energy performance is a Christmas staple, and no first-time holiday trip to New York is complete without it.

Day two: Central Park and Midtown Lights. Start the day with a stroll through Central Park. Head south to Wollman Rink (830 5th Ave) for a morning skate session with the Manhattan skyline as a backdrop. After that, take a leisurely walk through the park's snow-covered paths to admire the winter scenery, stopping at Bethesda Terrace and Bow Bridge for stunning views.

After lunch, visit the American Museum of Natural History (200 Central Park West) or The Metropolitan Museum of Art (1000 Fifth Avenue), both of which are beautifully decorated for the holidays. If you want a one-of-a-kind museum experience, visit the Met's medieval Christmas Tree and Neapolitan Baroque Crèche, a stunning nativity scene complete with lifelike figurines and angels.

In the evening, stroll down to Bryant Park (6th Avenue and 42nd Street) to explore the Winter Village. You'll find festive holiday markets, an ice rink, and warming stations where you can sip hot chocolate while browsing artisanal goods. The park's holiday tree is also illuminated during this time, adding to the magical atmosphere.

Day three - Brooklyn and Lower Manhattan On your final day, visit Dyker Heights in Brooklyn to see the city's most elaborate Christmas light displays. This neighbourhood, known for its extravagant holiday decorations, is best visited in the evening, but even during the day, you can admire the large-scale decorations that fill entire streets.

After exploring Brooklyn, return to Manhattan and visit Brookfield Place (230 Vesey St), where you can ice skate with views of the Hudson River and New York Harbor. End your day by visiting the One World Observatory at the One World Trade Center for breathtaking nighttime views of the city lit up by holiday lights.

10.2 A Family-Friendly Christmas Itinerary: Holiday Fun for the Kids

If you're travelling with children, this family-friendly itinerary will keep them entertained while you experience the magic of Christmas in New York. This three-day itinerary ensures a fun and memorable holiday trip for the entire family, from meeting Santa to viewing festive light displays.

Day one: Macy's Santaland and Times Square. Begin your family's Christmas adventure by visiting Macy's Santaland at Macy's Herald Square (151 W 34th St). Kids can meet Santa, explore the magical North Pole village, and even write a letter to him. To avoid long lines, reserve a time slot in advance.

After lunch, visit Times Square for a fun exploration of the giant billboards and holiday-themed stores such as M&M's World and the Disney Store. If your children enjoy theatre, consider seeing a family-friendly Broadway show like "The Lion King" or "Aladdin" to end the day with some musical magic.

Day two: Central Park, FAO Schwarz, and the Museum of Ice Cream Begin your second day with a trip to Central Park, where your children can burn off energy skating at Wollman Rink. Skate aids are available for younger children, making it a family-friendly activity. After skating, explore the park's playgrounds and perhaps take a horse-drawn carriage ride around the southern loop to add a fairytale element to your visit.

In the afternoon, go to FAO Schwarz at 30 Rockefeller Plaza to experience the iconic toy store. Allow your children to play on the giant piano or browse the extensive collection of toys, games, and stuffed animals. If you have time, visit the nearby Museum of Ice Cream in SoHo for a colourful, interactive experience where the entire family can enjoy sweet treats and playful exhibits.

Day three: Brooklyn Lights and Holiday Markets. On your final day, take your family on a Christmas light tour through Dyker Heights in Brooklyn. The extravagant light displays and inflatable decorations will captivate children of all ages. Consider booking a guided tour to make getting around the neighbourhood easier and more enjoyable.

Then, return to Manhattan and visit Bryant Park's Winter Village. The holiday markets here are ideal for finding unique Christmas gifts, and the family can relax with hot chocolate and snacks while watching the festive skating performances on the ice rink.

10.3 Romantic Christmas in NYC: Intimate Activities for Couples.

Romance reigns supreme in New York City during the holiday season. From cosy carriage rides to intimate dinners, this itinerary provides the ideal balance of iconic experiences and hidden gems for couples looking to spend a romantic Christmas getaway in the city.

Day One: Ice Skating and Fifth Avenue Stroll Begin your romantic getaway with a morning skate at The Rink at Rockefeller Center. Nothing is more iconic than gliding hand in hand beneath the Christmas tree and the surrounding skyscrapers. To make the experience even more memorable, book a VIP Skate package that includes exclusive rink access and a cosy warm-up session with hot chocolate following your skate.

After that, enjoy a stroll down Fifth Avenue, admiring the beautifully decorated window displays. Visit Tiffany & Co. at 727 5th Ave. to browse the jewellery—or even select something special for your loved one. For lunch, visit La Grenouille at 3 E 52nd St, a traditional French restaurant known for its romantic ambience and holiday charm.

In the evening, watch the Radio City Christmas Spectacular at Radio City Music Hall. The vibrant performance, complete with the Rockettes, is a must-see, and the festive spirit will have you both feeling swept away by the magic of the season.

Day two: Central Park and Upper East Side Elegance. Start the second day with a horse-drawn carriage ride through Central Park. When covered in snow, the park becomes a serene and magical setting, ideal for a romantic morning. Afterwards, go to The Met Cloisters on the Upper East Side to explore medieval art and gardens in a quiet, intimate setting.

Daniel, located at 60 E 65th St, offers an upscale dining experience for dinner. This Michelin-starred restaurant serves exquisite French cuisine, ideal for a special evening out. Make a reservation well in advance because it is one of the city's most popular dining spots.

Day three: Brooklyn Bridge and Rooftop Toast. On your final day, go to Brooklyn Heights and walk along the Brooklyn Heights Promenade. Sunset provides particularly stunning views of the Manhattan skyline and the Brooklyn Bridge. After your walk, cross the Brooklyn Bridge for a memorable New York City experience.

For your final evening, head to The Rooftop at Pier 17 in the Seaport District, where you can snuggle up with blankets and sip a warm drink while admiring the East River and Brooklyn Bridge. To cap off your romantic evening, eat dinner at The Fulton, a seafood restaurant on Pier 17 with stunning views and delectable cuisine.

Designing Your Perfect NYC Christmas Experience

Whether you're visiting New York for the first time, travelling with family, or planning a romantic getaway, these itineraries will ensure that you see everything the city has to offer during the holiday season.

From ice skating at iconic rinks to exploring enchanting neighbourhoods decked out in lights and decorations, there are plenty of magical moments to be had in New York during the holiday season. In the following chapter, we'll provide practical tips for navigating the city during the busy holiday season, allowing you to make the most of your trip with ease.

Practical Tips for Holiday

Travelling to New York City during the holiday season is a magical experience, but it also presents a few challenges due to increased crowds, festive events, and cold weather. To help make your trip as smooth and enjoyable as possible, this chapter provides essential tips for navigating the city, avoiding peak times at popular attractions, and staying warm in New York's winter weather.

11.1 Getting Around the City During the Holidays: Transportation Tips

New York City is well-known for its robust public transportation system, and navigating it effectively is critical during the busy holiday season. The subway is still the most efficient way to get around the city, especially when the streets are congested with holiday shoppers and tourists. To avoid long lines at ticket booths, consider purchasing a MetroCard in advance or using OMNY, a contactless payment system that allows you to enter subway stations by tapping your credit card or smartphone. Subway trains operate 24 hours a day, but some lines may experience delays or schedule changes during peak holiday periods, particularly around Thanksgiving and Christmas Eve.

Taxis and ridesharing services such as Uber and Lyft are widely available, but they can be expensive and slow during the holidays, particularly in Midtown Manhattan. If you intend to take a taxi or rideshare, expect delays and higher fares during rush hours or after major events such as the Radio City Christmas Spectacular or the Rockefeller Center tree lighting. Walking is frequently the quickest way to get around congested areas like Fifth Avenue and Times Square, and it allows you to fully appreciate the festive decorations and holiday window displays along the way.

Walking is often the most convenient option for short distances in tourist hotspots, and it's a great way to experience the city's holiday atmosphere. If you plan to visit several neighbourhoods, consider taking the NYC Ferry for a scenic ride between Lower Manhattan, Brooklyn, and the East River waterfront. The ferry provides stunning views of the city skyline and costs the same as a subway ride, making it a relaxing and cost-effective alternative to the subway.

If you plan to attend holiday events such as the Macy's Thanksgiving Day Parade or the New Year's Eve ball drop in Times Square, expect street closures and heavy pedestrian traffic. These events draw large crowds, and roads in and around event areas are frequently closed for hours, so plan your routes carefully and allow extra time to reach your destination.

11.2 Best Time to Visit Popular Attractions: Avoiding Crowds

New York City's holiday attractions attract large crowds, so planning your visits ahead of time can make all the difference. To avoid long lines and crowded venues, plan your days around the least busy times.

Rockefeller Center, with its iconic Christmas tree and ice skating rink, is one of the most popular holiday destinations in the city. To enjoy the tree and skating without feeling overwhelmed by crowds, go early in the morning (before 10 a.m.) or late at night (after 10 p.m.). Weekdays are generally less crowded than weekends, and visiting near the tree lighting ceremony in late November or early December will be more peaceful than the days leading up to Christmas. If you want to skate at The Rink at Rockefeller Center, make sure to reserve your time slot in advance, as it frequently sells out during peak hours.

Similarly, *Bryant Park's Winter Village* is a popular holiday destination, complete with an ice rink and a holiday market. The best time to go is early on a weekday morning when the rink is less crowded and the holiday shops have just opened. Afternoons and weekends are especially busy, as tourists and locals gather to enjoy the evening lights.

If you're going to see The Rockettes at Radio City or a Broadway show, consider booking a matinee performance. Matinees are less crowded and allow you to spend your evenings dining or sightseeing. For Broadway shows, try to book tickets on weekdays (Tuesday through Thursday), as weekend performances tend to sell out quickly and draw larger crowds.

If you're visiting museums like the **Metropolitan Museum of Art or the American Museum of Natural History**, go on weekday mornings or evenings when they have extended hours (usually Fridays or Saturdays). Avoid visiting on weekends or between Christmas and New Year's, when the city's museums are crowded with both locals and tourists.

Finally, for the best Christmas light displays in **Dyker Heights**, go after dusk on weekdays (around 6 p.m.), when the lights are fully lit. Weekends in December are especially congested with traffic and large tour groups, so visiting earlier in the week will allow you to see the spectacular displays without the crowds.

11.3 Winter Weather in New York: Packing for the Cold

New York winters can be cold, with temperatures dropping below freezing in December and January, and occasional snowfall adding to the festive atmosphere. Packing the appropriate winter gear is essential for staying comfortable while exploring the city.

Start with a warm winter coat that can withstand temperatures ranging from the mid-40s (Fahrenheit) to the 20s. A waterproof or water-resistant coat is recommended because rain, snow, and sleet are common in New York during the winter. Layering is essential, so bring thermal shirts or lightweight sweaters that are easy to put on and take off as you move between outdoor attractions and heated indoor venues.

Scarves, hats, and gloves are essential for staying warm, especially when walking long distances or waiting for outdoor events such as tree lightings or holiday performances. A good pair of insulated gloves will keep your hands warm, and a wool or fleece hat will prevent heat from escaping your head.

When it comes to footwear, waterproof boots with good traction are strongly recommended. Sidewalks can be slippery with ice or snow, so wear comfortable shoes that will keep your feet dry and warm. If you plan on spending the entire day outside, bring an extra pair of socks because your feet can get cold quickly when temperatures drop.

If you plan to attend outdoor events, bring hand warmers or foot warmers, which are inexpensive and can be easily slipped into your gloves or boots to provide extra warmth. Umbrellas are useful, but in harsh winter winds, a hooded coat may be preferable.

For those attending formal holiday dinners or shows, you can still dress up while staying warm by layering underneath your outfit and bringing a stylish coat or jacket to wear over it. Keep a small, foldable tote in your bag for any extra layers you might want to remove once inside.

Finally, while winter weather in New York can be unpredictable, coming prepared with the right gear will allow you to enjoy the holiday season in comfort and style, no matter how cold it gets.

Navigating NYC's Holiday Season with Ease

While New York's holiday season is undeniably busy, with a little planning and preparation, you can easily navigate the city's bustling streets, crowded attractions, and winter weather. You can fully enjoy the magic of a New York City Christmas without stress by taking advantage of off-peak times, using public transportation, and dressing warmly. In the following chapter, we'll discuss how to budget for your holiday trip, from low-cost dining options to free festive activities, so you can make the most of your visit without breaking the bank.

Sustainable Christmas Travel

As New York City transforms into a holiday wonderland, we must consider how we can enjoy the season responsibly. The holiday season is often associated with a lot of waste and excessive consumption, but there are many ways to make your trip to New York eco-friendly while still experiencing the festive magic. From sustainable shopping and dining to green holiday activities, this chapter will show you how to have a more sustainable and responsible Christmas in the city.

12.1 Eco-Friendly Holiday Tips for Sustainable Shopping and Dining

During the holiday season, shopping and dining take centre stage, and making more sustainable choices can help reduce the environmental impact of the celebrations. Fortunately, New York City provides numerous opportunities to support sustainable businesses and make environmentally friendly decisions, even during the holiday season.

Sustainable shopping

While it may be tempting to splurge on Christmas gifts and souvenirs, consider supporting local, eco-conscious businesses instead. SoHo and Brooklyn have a variety of boutiques and stores that prioritize sustainability. Look for stores that sell ethically produced items, such as those that use recycled materials, fair trade practices, or locally sourced products.

One of the best places to begin is **Package Free Shop** in Brooklyn (116 N 11th St, Brooklyn, NY 11249). This store aims to reduce waste by providing plastic-free, zero-waste products that are both functional and fashionable. From reusable kitchen items to eco-friendly beauty products, you'll find thoughtful gifts that reflect sustainable values.

Another option is **ABC Carpet & Home** (888 Broadway, New York, NY 10003), which sells artisan goods made from reclaimed materials. Their beautiful home décor, textiles, and ornaments make ideal holiday gifts that promote responsible sourcing and fair trade.

If you're looking for fashion, check out **Reformation** (39 Bond St, New York, NY 10012) or Everlane (28 Prince St, New York, NY 10012), both of which promote sustainable fabrics and ethical production methods. Their clothing collections are fashionable, high-quality, and made with minimal environmental impact, making them ideal for gifting or treating yourself during the holidays.

Environmentally Friendly Dining

New York City's food scene is as diverse as its population, and more restaurants are focusing on sustainability by serving locally sourced, organic, and plant-based options. One standout is ABC Kitchen (35 E 18th St, New York, NY 10003), which serves seasonal, farm-to-table dishes made with locally and sustainably grown ingredients. Dining here not only provides an excellent meal but also promotes environmentally friendly farming practices.

For a plant-based meal, visit Jajaja Plantas Mexicana (162 E Broadway, New York, NY 10002). This vegan Mexican restaurant serves delicious, innovative dishes made from plant-based ingredients, providing a more sustainable alternative to traditional dining. Their vibrant, flavorful menu is ideal for eco-conscious diners who want to enjoy holiday meals without contributing to the environmental impact of animal agriculture.

Van Leeuwen Ice Cream (48 ½ E 7th St, New York, NY 10003) offers vegan ice cream flavours made with natural, non-dairy ingredients to satisfy your sweet tooth. Not only are their treats delicious, but the company is dedicated to using high-quality, ethically sourced ingredients, allowing you to indulge guilt-free during your holiday trip.

12.2 Green Christmas Activities: Promoting Local and Sustainable Marketplaces

Participating in activities that support local artisans, businesses, and eco-friendly markets is an excellent way to embrace a sustainable holiday experience in New York. The city's holiday markets provide an excellent opportunity to shop sustainably while enjoying festive outdoor activities.

Union Square's Holiday Market

The Union Square Holiday Market, located in Union Square Park at 14th Street and Broadway, is a great place to find locally made, environmentally friendly gifts. Many of the market's vendors are small business owners and artisans who value ethical manufacturing practices. Whether you're looking for handcrafted jewellery, organic skincare products, or eco-friendly home décor, the Union Square Holiday Market has a wide range of unique, thoughtful gift ideas that align with your sustainability goals.

One of this market's distinguishing features is its emphasis on promoting local businesses and artisans. Shopping here benefits the local economy while lowering the carbon footprint associated with mass-produced goods. Look for vendors who use recycled materials, offer eco-friendly packaging, or sell fair trade items. The market typically runs from mid-November to Christmas Eve, giving you plenty of time to find environmentally friendly gifts.

Bryant Park Winter Village

The Winter Village at Bryant Park (6th Avenue and 42nd Street) is another holiday market that promotes sustainability. In addition to its festive ice rink, the Winter Village features over 170 boutique-style shops, many of which specialize in handmade and sustainable products. From artisanal food to upcycled jewellery, this market is ideal for those looking to shop ethically while enjoying the holiday spirit.

For foodies, Bryant Park has a variety of locally sourced and organic food stalls where you can indulge in treats made with fresh, seasonal ingredients. Whether you're looking for a snack or a more substantial meal, you can rest assured that many of the vendors are dedicated to sustainability and responsible sourcing.

Brooklyn Flea Holiday Market

The Brooklyn Flea Holiday Market is a must-see for anyone interested in exploring Brooklyn's vibrant artisan community. This market, located at 80 Pearl St, Brooklyn, NY 11201, sells a variety of vintage and handmade items, such as clothing, artwork, and home furnishings. Shopping vintage or secondhand is one of the most sustainable ways to reduce waste and extend product life cycles, so this market is ideal for finding one-of-a-kind gifts with minimal environmental impact.

Furthermore, many of the artisans at the Brooklyn Flea Holiday Market prioritize sustainability by using environmentally friendly materials or repurposing old items into new creations. It's an excellent way to support local artisans while reducing your holiday footprint.

Walk through NYC's green spaces.

Spending time in New York's many parks and green spaces allows you to enjoy the city's natural beauty while also practising sustainability. Taking a walk through Central Park, Prospect Park, or along the High Line is a great way to connect with nature and enjoy the holidays without depleting resources. These parks frequently host events such as winter nature walks, and you can learn about the city's efforts to keep public spaces sustainable, such as the High Line's eco-friendly design.

Celebrating Christmas responsibly in NYC

A sustainable holiday season in New York is not only feasible but also beneficial. You can experience the magic of Christmas in a way that is consistent with your values by supporting local artisans, shopping at eco-friendly markets, and dining at restaurants that prioritize sustainability. Whether you're looking for handmade gifts, eating plant-based meals, or simply enjoying the city's beautiful green spaces, you'll find countless ways to make your vacation memorable and environmentally conscious. In the next chapter, we'll look at how to budget for a New York City Christmas trip, from low-cost accommodations to free festive activities that won't break the bank.

Photography Hotspots: Capturing the Christmas Spirit in NYC

During the Christmas season, New York City is a photographer's paradise, with its festive lights, towering Christmas trees, and wintry landscapes providing endless opportunities to capture the holiday spirit. From iconic landmarks to hidden gems, this chapter will show you the best places for Christmas photos and give you advice on how to make the most of New York's dazzling holiday displays.

13.1 Best Places for Christmas Photos: Rockefeller Tree, Central Park, and More

Whether you're taking professional photos or capturing memories on your smartphone, New York's holiday hotspots make ideal backdrops for Christmas photos. The following are some of the most iconic and picturesque locations to photograph during the holiday season.

Rockefeller Center's Christmas Tree No holiday photo album is complete without a picture of the Rockefeller Center Christmas Tree. Located at 45 Rockefeller Plaza, New York, NY 10111, this iconic tree, illuminated with thousands of sparkling lights, serves as one of the city's most recognizable backdrops. The best time to photograph the tree is either early in the morning, before the crowds arrive, or late at night when the tree's lights are most visible against the dark sky.

For a unique perspective, head to the Top of the Rock Observation Deck, where you can see the tree and the surrounding plaza from above. The city skyline adds drama to your photos, and the panoramic views from the deck make excellent backdrops for portraits or wide shots.

During the Christmas season, Central Park transforms into a winter wonderland, complete with snow-covered paths, frozen lakes, and iconic landmarks. Head to Wollman Rink (830 5th Ave, New York, NY 10065) to photograph skaters gliding beneath the Manhattan skyline. The early morning light is especially beautiful here, casting a soft glow on the ice.

The Bethesda Terrace and Fountain are also excellent photography locations. When snow falls, the stone steps and arches take on a magical, old-world charm, resulting in breathtaking winter portraits. Bow Bridge, one of the park's most romantic locations, is also ideal for photographing snow-covered landscapes or intimate couple portraits.

Fifth Avenue Holiday Displays The holiday window displays along Fifth Avenue are an annual tradition in New York, with stores such as Saks Fifth Avenue and Bergdorf Goodman creating intricate, themed displays that captivate both day and night. If you want to photograph the displays during the day, try to shoot early in the morning to avoid crowds. At night, the lights on the storefronts cast a lovely glow, making ideal conditions for festive photos.

For a complete view of Saks Fifth Avenue's synchronized light show, walk across the street to the Rockefeller Center Channel Gardens. The light show occurs every 10 minutes after sunset, and from this vantage point, you can photograph both the building's glittering façade and the crowd's reaction.

Dyker Heights Christmas Lights Dyker Heights in Brooklyn is the place to go if you want to see extravagant Christmas decorations. This neighbourhood, located between 11th and 13th Avenues and 83rd to 86th Streets, is well-known for its extravagant holiday lights and displays. Bring your camera at dusk, when the lights begin to turn on and photograph the homes decorated with inflatable Santas, life-size reindeer, and glowing holiday scenes.

To photograph the lights at Dyker Heights, use a wide-angle lens to capture the full scale of the displays or a telephoto lens for close-ups of more intricate details. Because this area can become crowded with visitors, consider visiting on a weekday evening to get fewer people in your photos.

Brooklyn Bridge and Dumbo The Brooklyn Bridge and the DUMBO neighbourhood make excellent backdrops for iconic holiday photos. From Pebble Beach in Brooklyn Bridge Park, you can photograph the bridge with the Manhattan skyline in the background. During the holiday season, the lights on the skyline and bridge add a festive touch to your photographs.

In DUMBO, head to the corner of Washington Street and Front Street for a perfect shot of the Manhattan Bridge framed by the neighbourhood's brick buildings. The bridge's twinkling lights in the distance make for a striking holiday photo, especially during golden hour or after dark.

13.2 Guidelines for Photographing New York's Holiday Lights and Decorations

Capturing the magic of New York's holiday lights and decorations can be a rewarding challenge, especially when balancing bright lights against dark winter evenings. Here are some practical tips that will help you achieve the best results:

1. Use a tripod for nighttime shots. Holiday lights and decorations are best photographed in low light, and camera stabilization is essential to avoid blurry images. When shooting at night, a tripod is essential, especially if you're using a lower ISO or a longer exposure. With a stable setup, you can shoot longer exposures to capture the entire glow of the lights without worrying about camera shake.

2. Adjust your ISO settings. When shooting in low light, you'll need to adjust your ISO to avoid dark or grainy images. Start with an ISO of 400 to 800 and adjust as needed. Be aware that increasing the ISO too high can introduce noise into your images, so choose the lowest setting that still allows enough light in for a sharp photo.

3. Use a Fast Lens to Improve Night Performance. A fast lens (one with a low f-stop, such as f/1.8 or f/2.8) can help you capture more light, allowing you to shoot better photos in low-light conditions. A wide aperture also produces a shallow depth of field, causing the holiday lights to blend into a beautiful, bokeh-filled background behind your subject.

4. Experiment with exposure times. Experiment with different exposure times to capture the glow of holiday lights. Longer exposures (1-2 seconds) allow you to capture the vibrancy of the lights while keeping the surrounding scenery visible. However, do not overexpose the lights, as this can cause them to lose detail. Begin with shorter exposures and gradually increase the duration as necessary.

5. Focus on details. While wide shots of Christmas lights can be stunning, don't overlook the small details that make the holidays special. Zoom in on window displays, intricate decorations, or individual ornaments to highlight the craftsmanship and creativity that go into New York's holiday displays.

6. Capture Reflections During the winter, New York's streets are often covered in rain or snow, and you can take advantage of these reflective surfaces. Look for puddles or wet sidewalks that reflect the holiday lights or tree decorations. Reflections add drama to your shots, making them stand out.

7. *Timing is everything*. For outdoor light displays, try to shoot during "blue hour," which is just after sunset but before the sky completely darkens. During this time, the sky is a deep blue, creating the ideal backdrop for twinkling holiday lights. This period typically lasts between 30-45 minutes, so plan your shoot accordingly.

8. *Remember to Include People*. Including people in your holiday photos can add warmth and scale to your images. Whether it's a family skating at Wollman Rink or a couple admiring the Rockefeller Christmas Tree, candid moments make for unforgettable and emotional holiday photos.

Capturing the Spirit of Christmas in NYC.

New York City is one of the most photogenic cities in the world, and during the holiday season, its lights and decorations provide endless opportunities for stunning photos. Whether you're photographing the grandeur of the Rockefeller Christmas Tree or the intimate beauty of a snow-covered Central Park, these locations and tips will help you capture the holiday magic in New York City. In the next chapter, we'll look at how to budget for a New York City Christmas trip, from low-cost accommodations to free festive activities that won't break the bank.

NYC Beyond Christmas: Celebrating New Year's Eve

While Christmas in New York is magical, the city truly comes alive on New Year's Eve. From the iconic Times Square Ball Drop to dazzling firework displays and vibrant parties, New York has a variety of ways to ring in the new year in style. Whether you want to party in Times Square or have a more intimate celebration with breathtaking views, this chapter will walk you through the best ways to welcome 2025 in the city that never sleeps.

14.1 Times Square Ball Drop: What to Expect on New Year's Eve

The Times Square Ball Drop is one of the world's most famous New Year's Eve celebrations, with millions of people watching in person and via live broadcasts. This celebration, held in Manhattan's Times Square, has been a tradition since 1907, making it an iconic way to end the year.

If you're planning on attending the Times Square Ball Drop, plan to arrive early. Crowds gather as early as noon on New Year's Eve to secure a spot, even though the main events do not begin until the evening. The earlier you arrive, the better your chances of getting a good view of the stage, which will feature live performances by popular artists throughout the evening. As the night progresses, the iconic New Year's Eve Ball—a 12-foot geodesic sphere covered in nearly 2,700 Waterford Crystal triangles—will descend from the top of One Times Square, signalling the final countdown to midnight.

What to Expect

Security and safety: Due to the large crowds, security is strict. Attendees must pass through metal detectors, and large bags, alcohol, and umbrellas are not permitted. It is critical to pack light and dress warmly, as temperatures can be quite cold, especially given the long wait outside.

Viewing the Ball Drop: The best viewing areas are typically on Broadway between 43rd and 50th Streets and on 7th Avenue between 43rd and 59th Streets. Keep in mind that once you enter the viewing area, you will not be able to leave or return, so plan on staying in your spot overnight.

Entertainment: The evening begins with live musical performances, celebrity appearances, and speeches. As midnight approaches, the excitement builds with the famous countdown to the new year, culminating in the iconic ball drop and confetti shower over Times Square.

While the Times Square Ball Drop is an unforgettable experience, the large crowds and long wait times can be overwhelming. If you're looking for a more relaxed or unconventional way to celebrate, New York has plenty of exciting options for welcoming the new year.

14.2 Best Places to Celebrate New Year's in the City: Fireworks and Festivities

Beyond Times Square, New York City has a variety of New Year's Eve celebrations to choose from, including intimate gatherings with breathtaking views and public events featuring fireworks. Here are some of the best places to celebrate the new year in the city.

1. Central Park Fireworks and Midnight Run For a more relaxed and family-friendly New Year's Eve celebration, Central Park is an excellent choice. The park hosts a midnight fireworks display, and there is plenty of room to spread out, making it much less crowded than Times Square. The fireworks are launched from Bow Bridge, near Cherry Hill, and provide spectacular views of the park.

The New York Road Runners Midnight Run is a festive 4-mile race that starts at 10 p.m. and lasts until midnight. Participants are treated to fireworks and live music along the course, making it a fun and active way to start the new year.

2. New Year's Eve in Prospect Park. Prospect Park in Brooklyn hosts its own free, family-friendly fireworks celebration. The event, held at Grand Army Plaza, features live music, hot chocolate, and a spectacular midnight fireworks display. This is an excellent choice for those who want to avoid the Manhattan crowds while still experiencing a festive atmosphere.

Long Meadow offers the best view of the fireworks, with the vibrant display lighting up the sky. Arriving early is recommended because the event attracts a sizable local crowd, but it's much more manageable than Times Square.

3. Fireworks on the Brooklyn Bridge For a romantic and scenic celebration, visit DUMBO or Brooklyn Bridge Park and watch fireworks over the Brooklyn Bridge. This area provides breathtaking views of the city skyline, bridge, and harbour, making it one of New York's most picturesque New Year's Eve destinations.

Many local restaurants and rooftop bars in DUMBO provide special New Year's Eve packages that include dinner, drinks, and prime viewing spots for the midnight fireworks. For a casual and free option, walk along the waterfront or the Brooklyn Heights Promenade to get a great view of the show.

4. Boat Cruises in New York Harbor. Consider booking a New Year's Eve cruise around New York Harbor for a truly one-of-a-kind celebration. Several boat companies provide all-inclusive packages that include dinner, dancing, and unlimited drinks as you cruise past New York's most iconic landmarks, such as the Statue of Liberty and the Brooklyn Bridge.

At midnight, you'll have front-row seats for multiple fireworks displays from the water, providing an unforgettable way to start the new year. Circle Line, Hornblower, and Classic Harbor Line are popular options, so compare packages and book early to secure a spot.

5. Rooftop bars with views of the skyline. New York's skyline is at its most dazzling on New Year's Eve, and there's no better place to enjoy the view than from a rooftop bar. Several high-rise hotels and lounges host New Year's Eve parties with panoramic views of the city, including prime locations for viewing the Times Square Ball Drop from afar.

One popular option is 230 **Fifth Rooftop Bar** (230 5th Ave, New York, NY 10001), which offers heated igloos and breathtaking views of the Empire State Building. Their New Year's Eve party features drinks, hors d'oeuvres, and dancing, making it an excellent choice for those looking to celebrate in style while avoiding the crowds below.

The Skylark, located at 200 W 39th St, is another excellent rooftop bar for a stylish celebration, with stunning views of Midtown Manhattan and the Hudson River. This upscale venue hosts a glamorous New Year's Eve celebration with cocktails, live music, and breathtaking city views.

Celebrating the New Year in Style.

Whether you're braving the crowds in Times Square, watching fireworks from a Brooklyn park, or dancing the night away on a harbour cruise, New York has countless ways to celebrate New Year's Eve. From intimate gatherings to grand celebrations, there is something for everyone as the city welcomes 2025 with fireworks, music, and joy. Regardless of where you choose to celebrate, you will be a part of one of the world's most iconic New Year's Eve celebrations, making memories to last a lifetime. In the following chapter, we will look at how to budget for your New York Christmas and New Year's trip, from low-cost accommodations to free festive activities that won't break the bank.

Budget Breakdown for Visiting New York City During Christmas 2024

Planning a trip to New York City during the holiday season is an exciting but potentially expensive endeavour. From accommodation to transportation and dining, the costs can add up quickly, especially during the peak Christmas and New Year's period. In this chapter, we will provide a detailed and accurate cost breakdown for visiting New York City in December 2024, covering all major expenses such as accommodation, transportation, dining, activities, and more. This guide will help you plan and budget effectively to make the most of your holiday trip without breaking the bank.

15.1 Accommodation Costs

Accommodation is likely to be your largest expense, especially during the holiday season when demand is at its highest. New York City offers a wide range of options, from budget hotels to luxury stays, so your costs will depend on the type of experience you are seeking.

Budget Hotels (2-3 stars)

For budget travellers, there are several affordable hotel options in areas like Midtown Manhattan, Queens, and Brooklyn. Expect basic amenities and smaller rooms, but proximity to key attractions.

Average nightly rate: $150 to $250

Estimated cost for a 5-night stay: $750 to $1,250

Examples of budget hotels

➢ Pod 51 Hotel (Midtown East): Rooms start at around $180 per night.
➢ LIC Hotel (Queens): Rates range from $150 to $220 per night, with easy access to Manhattan via subway.

Mid-Range Hotels (3-4 stars)

Mid-range hotels offer a balance of comfort, amenities, and location. These hotels are often located in prime areas such as Times Square, Chelsea, and the Upper West Side. Expect slightly larger rooms and better facilities.

➢ Average nightly rate: $250 to $400
➢ Estimated cost for a 5-night stay: $1,250 to $2,000

Examples of mid-range hotels

➢ The Hotel @ Times Square: Rates typically range from $280 to $350 per night.
➢ Moxy NYC Times Square: Offers rooms for around $300 per night, with stylish amenities and a great location.

Luxury Hotels (5 stars)

If you're looking for a luxurious holiday experience, New York's high-end hotels offer world-class service, spacious rooms, and breathtaking views, often located near iconic sites like Central Park, Fifth Avenue, and Rockefeller Center.

➢ Average nightly rate: $600 to $1,500 (and higher)
➢ Estimated cost for a 5-night stay: $3,000 to $7,500+

Examples of luxury hotels

➢ The Plaza Hotel: Prices start at around $1,000 per night.
➢ The Peninsula New York: Rates typically range from $900 to $1,400 per night.

15.2 Transportation Costs

New York City's public transportation system is extensive, making it relatively easy and affordable to get around the city. You can also opt for taxis or rideshare services, but these tend to be more expensive, especially during peak holiday times.

Public Transportation (Subway and Buses)

The subway is the most efficient and cost-effective way to travel across the city. The MTA MetroCard or OMNY system allows access to both the subway and buses.

➢ Single subway/bus ride: $2.90
➢ Unlimited weekly MetroCard: $34 (unlimited rides on subways and buses for 7 days)
➢ Estimated transportation cost for 5 days: $34 per person if using an unlimited MetroCard

Taxis and Rideshares (Uber/Lyft)

Taxis and rideshare services are convenient but more expensive during the holidays due to high demand and traffic congestion.

> ➤ An average taxi ride within Manhattan: $15 to $25 (short trips, including tip)
> ➤ Uber/Lyft: Prices vary, but you can expect to pay $15 to $30 for short rides and $40+ for longer trips or during peak times.
> ➤ Estimated rideshare costs for 5 days (assuming 2 rides per day): $150 to $250 depending on distance and surge pricing.

Airport Transfers

Getting to and from the airport is another consideration. Options include public transit, airport shuttles, taxis, or rideshare services.

> ➤ Subway from JFK Airport (AirTrain + Subway): $10.75 total
> ➤ Taxi from JFK to Manhattan: Flat rate of $70 (including tip and tolls)
> ➤ Uber/Lyft from JFK to Manhattan: $65 to $90 depending on time and traffic
> ➤ Shuttle services: $20 to $35 per person
> ➤ *Estimated airport transfer cost (round trip):*
> ➤ Public transport: $21 per person
> ➤ Taxi or rideshare: $130 to $180 (round trip)

15.3 Dining Costs

New York City offers a wide range of dining experiences, from cheap eats to Michelin-starred restaurants. Your daily dining budget will depend on the type of meals you prefer.

Budget Dining (Casual and Fast Food)

If you plan on eating at casual spots or enjoying street food, you can expect to spend less while still enjoying delicious meals.

➢ Breakfast: $5 to $10 (bagels, coffee, or grab-and-go options)
➢ Lunch: $10 to $20 (deli sandwiches, pizza slices, fast-casual chains)
➢ Dinner: $15 to $30 (diners, burger joints, or casual eateries)
➢ Estimated daily budget for budget dining: $30 to $60 per person
➢ 5-day total: $150 to $300 per person

Mid-Range Dining (Sit-Down Restaurants)

For those looking to enjoy New York's diverse food scene, mid-range restaurants offer a variety of cuisines at reasonable prices.

➢ Breakfast: $10 to $20 (brunch spots or cafés)
➢ Lunch: $20 to $30 (sit-down restaurants)
➢ Dinner: $30 to $50 (popular restaurants, gastropubs, or ethnic cuisine)

- ➤ Estimated daily budget for mid-range dining: $60 to $100 per person
- ➤ 5-day total: $300 to $500 per person

Fine Dining (Luxury Restaurants)

New York is home to some of the finest restaurants in the world. For those seeking a special holiday meal, expect to spend more on fine dining experiences.

- ➤ Breakfast/brunch: $20 to $50
- ➤ Lunch: $30 to $60
- ➤ Dinner: $75 to $150 (or more depending on the restaurant)
- ➤ Estimated daily budget for fine dining: $125 to $250 per person
- ➤ 5-day total: $625 to $1,250 per person

15.4 Activities and Entertainment Costs

New York City offers plenty of free activities during the holidays, such as viewing the Rockefeller Christmas Tree and window displays, but some iconic experiences come with costs.

Key Holiday Activities

- ➤ Radio City Christmas Spectacular: $49 to $275 per ticket
- ➤ Broadway Show: $49 to $250 per ticket
- ➤ Ice Skating at Rockefeller Center: $21 to $58 (plus $15 for skate rentals)

- ➢ Top of the Rock Observation Deck: $40 to $60 per person
- ➢ Empire State Building: $44 to $79 per person
- ➢ Metropolitan Museum of Art: Suggested donation, but $30 for adults is typical
- ➢ American Museum of Natural History: $28 per adult

Estimated cost for activities over 5 days:

- ➢ Budget: $200 to $300 per person (free activities, museum visits, ice skating)
- ➢ Mid-Range: $400 to $600 per person (Broadway show, Christmas Spectacular, museums)
- ➢ Luxury: $800 to $1,200 per person (premium tickets, fine dining, special events)

15.5 Miscellaneous Costs

Souvenirs: $50 to $200 depending on what you purchase (holiday ornaments, NYC memorabilia, etc.)

Tips: 15% to 20% of the bill at restaurants, $1 to $2 per bag for hotel bellhops, and $1 to $5 for housekeeping per day.

Phone/Data Plan: If you're visiting from outside the U.S., consider a local SIM card or roaming plan. Local SIM cards with data can cost around $30 to $50 for a week.

15.6 Total Estimated Cost for a 5-Day Trip

Budget Traveler

➢ Accommodation: $750 to $1,250
➢ Transportation: $34 (MetroCard) + $21 (airport transfer) = $55
➢ Dining: $150 to $300
➢ Activities: $200 to $300
➢ Miscellaneous: $100
➢ Total: $1,255 to $2,005

Mid-Range Traveler

➢ Accommodation: $1,250 to $2,000
➢ Transportation: $55 to $150
➢ Dining: $300 to $500
➢ Activities: $400 to $600
➢ Miscellaneous: $150
➢ Total: $2,155 to $3,400

Luxury Traveler

➢ Accommodation: $3,000 to $7,500
➢ Transportation: $150 to $250
➢ Dining: $625 to $1,250
➢ Activities: $800 to $1,200
➢ Miscellaneous: $200
➢ Total: $4,775 to $10,400+

Budgeting for a Magical NYC Christmas

Visiting New York City during Christmas 2024 can be tailored to any budget, whether you're looking for a luxury holiday experience or a more affordable adventure. By planning, securing deals, and balancing free activities with key paid experiences, you can enjoy all the magic of New York at Christmas without overspending. The estimated costs provided here will help you prepare financially for your trip, ensuring that your holiday season in New York is both magical and manageable.

Useful Contacts

When travelling to New York City, especially during the busy holiday season, it's important to have essential contact information and emergency numbers readily available. From tourist information centres to local emergency services, these resources will help ensure a smooth and safe trip.

Tourist Information Centers

NYC & Company Visitor Information Center

Address: 810 7th Ave, New York, NY 10019 (between 52nd and 53rd Streets)

Phone: +1 (212) 484-1222

Hours: Monday to Friday, 9:00 a.m. – 5:00 p.m. (Closed on weekends and public holidays)

Services: The official visitor information centre for New York City offers maps, brochures, and personalized advice from staff about sightseeing, events, and activities. You can also get help with booking tours or purchasing tickets to local attractions.

Times Square Museum & Visitor Center

Address: 1560 Broadway, New York, NY 10036 (between 46th and 47th Streets)

Phone: +1 (212) 452-5283

Hours: Monday to Sunday, 8:00 a.m. – 8:00 p.m.

Services: Located in the heart of Times Square, this visitor centre provides city guides, maps, and information on nearby attractions. It's a great stop if you're new to the city or looking for tips on the area.

Grand Central Terminal Information Booth

Address: 89 E 42nd St, New York, NY 10017 (Main Concourse)

Phone: +1 (212) 340-2583

Hours: Monday to Friday, 9:00 a.m. – 6:00 p.m.

Services: This centrally located information desk assists with directions, travel tips, and details about local landmarks.

Emergency Numbers

In case of emergencies, it's crucial to know the relevant numbers to call:

General Emergency Number (Fire, Police, Medical): 911

Available for any emergency, including accidents, crimes, or medical issues.

Non-Emergency Police Number: 311

For reporting non-emergency issues such as noise complaints, lost items, or city services, 311 is a useful resource for residents and visitors alike.

Closest Hospital – NewYork-Presbyterian/Weill Cornell Medical Center

Address: 525 E 68th St, New York, NY 10065

Phone: +1 (212) 746-5454

US State Department for Foreign Travelers

For foreign travellers, it's a good idea to contact your local consulate in case of any emergency involving passport issues, legal help, or other assistance.

US State Department: +1 (888) 407-4747

Poison Control: 1-800-222-1222

For poisoning emergencies, this nationwide hotline provides immediate advice on how to handle situations involving accidental ingestion or exposure to harmful substances.

Local Transportation Information

MTA (Metropolitan Transportation Authority) Subway and Buses

Phone: +1 (718) 330-1234

Website: www.mta.info

MTA offers information on subway and bus routes, schedules, and fare options, including the OMNY system and MetroCards.

Taxis and Car Services

NYC Yellow Taxi: Dial 311 for taxi information or hail one on the street.

Uber/Lyft: Available via their respective apps (downloadable from the App Store or Google Play).

16.2 Recommended Apps for NYC Christmas Travelers

Technology can greatly enhance your travel experience, particularly in a busy city like New York. From navigating public transportation to finding restaurants and keeping track of events, these apps are essential for making the most of your holiday trip.

Navigation and Transportation Apps

Google Maps

Platform: iOS and Android

Features: Provides detailed navigation for walking, driving, and public transportation routes across the city. It also offers real-time updates on traffic and subway delays.

Why It's Useful: Google Maps is a must-have for finding your way around New York's complex grid of streets, subways, and bus routes.

Citymapper

Platform: iOS and Android

Features: Offers real-time transit information for subways, buses, ferries, and rideshare services. Citymapper also shows step-by-step walking directions, subway entrances, and bike routes.

Why It's Useful: Citymapper is particularly helpful in New York City for planning multi-modal trips, finding the fastest routes, and tracking real-time public transportation updates.

MTA Subway Time

Platform: iOS and Android

Features: Offers real-time train arrival information for the NYC subway system, with updates on delays or service changes.

Why It's Useful: Ideal for navigating the subway efficiently, especially during busy holiday travel times.

Entertainment and Activity Planning Apps

Eventbrite

Platform: iOS and Android

Features: Helps you discover events, tours, and activities happening throughout the city. You can filter by category (Christmas events, concerts, markets, etc.) and book tickets directly through the app.

Why It's Useful: Eventbrite makes it easy to find and book tickets for festive holiday events, including Christmas markets, concerts, and seasonal performances.

TKTS

Platform: iOS and Android

Features: The app offers access to discounted same-day tickets for Broadway and off-Broadway shows.

Why It's Useful: TKTS is perfect for scoring last-minute deals on tickets to popular Broadway shows during the holiday season. The app lets you check ticket availability and purchase directly from your phone.

OpenTable

Platform: iOS and Android

Features: Allows you to discover and reserve tables at thousands of restaurants across New York City.

Why It's Useful: OpenTable is a great way to secure reservations at some of New York's best holiday dining spots, ensuring you avoid the long waits that often come with the busy holiday season.

Shopping and Market Apps

Christmas in New York

Platform: iOS and Android

Features: Offers a guide to the top holiday attractions, markets, and events happening in New York City during Christmas. It also highlights key shopping locations and Christmas tree lighting.

Why It's Useful: It provides a curated selection of festive events and activities, helping travellers navigate the holiday season's most iconic experiences.

ShopDrop

Platform: iOS and Android

Features: This app helps you discover sample sales and discounts at designer boutiques and high-end stores in New York.

Why It's Useful: ShopDrop is ideal for holiday shoppers who want to take advantage of special sales and discounts on fashion and accessories during their visit.

Weather and Safety Apps

AccuWeather

Platform: iOS and Android

Features: Provides accurate, real-time weather forecasts and updates. It includes radar maps, severe weather alerts, and hourly updates.

Why It's Useful: During winter in New York, it's important to stay informed about the weather, especially with the potential for snow or ice storms. AccuWeather ensures you're prepared for the cold.

Citizen

Platform: iOS and Android

Features: Provides real-time safety alerts based on your location, including information about nearby incidents or emergencies. It also includes updates on traffic conditions and street closures.

Why It's Useful: The Citizen app helps you stay aware of any nearby emergencies, making it easier to avoid crowded or unsafe areas, particularly during major events like the Times Square Ball Drop.

Language and Currency Apps

Google Translate

Platform: iOS and Android

Features: Offers instant translation for over 100 languages, including text, speech, and image translations.

Why It's Useful: While most people in New York speak English, the app is handy for non-native English speakers or international travellers navigating menus, and signs, or conversing with locals.

XE Currency

Platform: iOS and Android

Features: Provides up-to-date currency conversion rates for travellers.

Why It's Useful: For international travellers, XE Currency helps calculate expenses and understand exchange rates, especially when budgeting for shopping or dining.

Maps

New York city metropolitan

Tourist Map

Made in the USA
Las Vegas, NV
05 November 2024

11174977R00056